The Truth

I'm a girl, I'm smart, And I know Everything!

Dr. Barbara Becker Holstein

Enchanted Self Press
Long Branch, NJ
USA

Copyright ©2008
Dr. Barbara Becker Holstein

Printed in Canada
Library of Congress Cataloguing in Publication Data 2007920741
Barbara Becker Holstein, author

Cover and Interior design
by Gwyn Kennedy Snider

The Truth
ISBN 978-0-9798952-0-3

Dr. Barbara Becker Holstein, nationally known Positive Psychologist, is the creator of The Enchanted Self,® a systematic way of helping bring more joy, meaning, and purpose into our lives.

Dr. Holstein has been a school psychologist for over 25 years. She also taught first and second grades. She is in private practice as a psychologist, with her husband, Dr .Russell M. Holstein, for over 25 years, in Long Branch, New Jersey.

You can find Dr. Holstein on the web at www.enchantedself.com and can write to her at drbarbara@enchantedself.com.

Blog: www.thetruthforgirls.com

"All grownups were children first.
(But few of them remember it)."

"Grownups never understand anything by themselves,
and it is exhausting for children to provide explanations
over and over again."

From "The Little Prince"

Introduction to **THE TRUTH**

Barbara Becker Holstein, Ed.D.

When I was a girl I knew so many things. I knew a lot of important stuff that my parents and other grown-ups had forgotten. I promised myself that I would find a way to hold on to my knowledge.

Then I grew up and became a teacher and a psychologist. I got married and had children. At work, as a psychologist, I listen to a lot of people's problems, children and grown-ups. I always try to help them. One of the things I do is to point out to them what is right with them, rather than what is wrong. Another thing I do is to teach them how to have more fun. I also help them to remember their own wisdom and the truths that they already know in their hearts.

One day I decided to find a way to combine what I already knew as a girl with the knowledge I have as a psychologist. I had to find a fun way to do this that would really help girls and mothers recognize that what we know growing up is just as important as what we learn later.

One day, the 'girl' just appeared. She knew what to say and how to say it. She did a much better job of sharing **THE TRUTH** than I ever could have imagined. So I just let her go for it.

Here is her account of **THE TRUTH**. I hope you enjoy it. Remember your promises to yourself when you grow up and don't forget to listen to your kids someday.

I better get out of the way and let the girl begin......

This is my secret diary. Not the one that says "Girl Scout Diary." I leave that around just to fool grown-ups. This is the real truth. This is where I will write everything I don't want to forget, starting tomorrow!

The Truth

I'm a girl, I'm smart.
And I know Everything!

Dear Diary,

I am in love. I thought I would fall in love when I was much older, maybe 15 or 16. Not today.

I was sitting in class, reading a social studies chapter, trying to answer an awful question at the end of the chapter, "Which state has the most coal mines," when the door opened and a new kid walked in.

There he was! I knew as soon as I saw him. He was wearing a cute plaid shirt and he had brown hair and brown eyes.

My heart felt like it turned over in my body. My pulse started to race. I couldn't concentrate. I felt excited, like I suddenly had a big secret. "Our eyes locked." I read that in a book that my mom had by her bed. It was true. When I looked into his brown eyes, I felt we had known each other forever. Looking at him made me feel all fluttery inside.

I wanted him to sit near me so badly I could have died. But he sat in the row in front of me, a little to the right. Not too bad. Now I can look at him all day. My best friend, Angela, sits beside him, to his right. I hope she doesn't fall in love with him too. He's mine! His name is Paul.

1

Dear Diary,

How will I ever be able to think about school work again with all these funny feelings in my belly and my heart beating so fast I can't breathe?

I can't wait to go to school tomorrow. Now I know how girls fall in love. It happened to me today and I'm only 11. And that's the truth.

Dear Diary,

I have a secret. I want to know about growing up. I want to ask my mother questions, like when will I need a bra, but I can't. Whenever I try she always looks away and starts to fidget with her fingers. Then she will 'remember' that she has to cook supper or do the laundry and I never really get an answer to my questions. Why is that? Doesn't she know how confused I am? How am I supposed to be ready to get older if she can't even tell me what to expect? Sometimes I wish I was Mrs. Allen's daughter. That's Angela's mother. Mrs. Allen tells Angela everything she needs to know. Angela is so lucky and that's the truth. I'm a little lucky because at least I get some of my questions answered second hand.

I'm worried. How will I know who else to marry if I can't marry Paul?

How will that ever happen? I couldn't stand to be alone as a grownup, and I would die if I couldn't have children. My dolls are my babies. I sleep with Cookie and Cuddles. They wear six-month size baby clothes. Cuddles has holes in her nose and breathes when you press her stomach.

I love them so much!

Dear Diary,

I hate my mother sometimes. We were on the back porch and I finally asked her how will I know when I need a bra? She just walked back into the kitchen saying, "You're too young. I didn't think about things like that at your age. You should be out playing or doing chores"

I shouldn't have bothered. Maybe Angela can ask her mother. I feel so angry inside. I hope I can sleep tonight. Why can't my mother just talk to me?

Dear Diary,

Yesterday my father's cousin George came to visit from Las Vegas, where he lives. He stayed for lunch and then we took him to the Lake and then we went to Howard Johnson's for supper and my parents treated him. After we came home, we sat in the living room for a long time. He talked and talked. That would have been OK, except he swore the whole time. He'd say a few words and then he would mix in a swear word. I can't even write them, you'll just have to believe me. For example, he would say, "and what the h—— do you think of that, Edith?" My mom would just answer as if he hadn't sworn. Then he would go on and swear again.

Every time he swore it gave me a bad feeling in my stomach. I asked him not to swear, but he just laughed at me as if he knew more than I do. But the truth is I know more than he does. Swearing makes the whole room feel heavy, as if little arrows are being shot off, hitting people and hurting them. Either he doesn't know the truth or he doesn't care.

Dear Diary,

My parents didn't seem that bothered. What happens to grown-ups that they don't seem to care anymore to make the world a beautiful place?

When I got up this morning, I was so glad that George wasn't here anymore.

Grown-ups say they know so much about life, but I know more. I know swearing is bad for all of us, and that's the truth.

Dear Diary,

I have a lot of courage. I don't mind talking to strangers.
One day my mom and I were in the Big Top restaurant
downtown and I had just ordered a delicious cheeseburger
with French fries. Across the room I saw a very big-shot
man. He was the boss where my dad works, so I just
jumped out of my seat, left my mother, and went up to him.

I said, "Hi!" and held out my hand for him to shake it.

He smiled such a giant smile and said he was so happy I
had come over and how brave I was. He looked around to
see if I was with anyone, and of course my mother was
sitting at the table. He walked me back and
said to Mom, "My, what a bright, friendly
child you have."

I was so happy with myself. My heart was
beating fast and I knew that when I was
a grown-up I would be just like that: brave,
daring, not afraid to meet people.

Dear Diary,

Today was the best day ever. My father took us on one of our Mystery Rides. I love them. We get in the car after lunch and then we each get turns directing him. I had the first turn, so I said, "Go straight for two miles." And then my mother said, "Take a right, a left, a right, and a left, and then go straight for one mile." We kept on having turns and laughing our heads off as we went by the craziest places. We went by the city dump, the hospital, and lots of funeral homes, and we ended up in a big park.

Finally Daddy called time out and we stopped and he took over. Then we had to close our eyes until he told us to open them. When we did, we were near our house, at a drug store that sells the BEST ice cream cones. So we all got out, went in, and had ice cream. I got a coffee cone with sprinkles. I loved it.

The best times are the fun times, when no one is fighting and we all get turns and we all get treats. And that's the truth!

Dear Diary,

My brother is so dumb. He started to cry. I asked him why he was crying. He told me that he thought that he was the only one that saw colors inside his eyes when he closes his eyes. He said, "I thought I was special."

Today he found out that Billy down the street sees lots of colors too.

How dumb can a six year old get?

But I didn't tell him that. I just gave him a hug, got him a Kleenex and a Hostess cupcake out of the cabinet.

After all, I am the big sister!

Dear Diary,

Why does Betsy hate me? She's so mean to me. I think she talks about me when I walk by. In fact, I'm sure of it, and I know she is saying not-nice things. Once I saw her point at my skirt and laugh at the same time. Then the other girls with her started to laugh.

Maybe I grew this year and my skirt is a tiny bit short. I feel awful. And to top it off, her big brother pushed me at the playground for no good reason when he walked by me. I fell backwards and hit my head on the brick wall of the school. I had to stay in the nurse's office with an ice bag on my head for the rest of the afternoon. And my head still hurts a little. They hate me! I hate them!

My mother told me to ignore them. I'm trying to, but they make me feel like I have cooties, like something is wrong with me. I want to have lots of friends.

The truth is people shouldn't make fun of you. It really hurts.

11

Dear Diary,

Here's what I do all by myself. I catch the bus two blocks from my house and go downtown. I'm not afraid. My mother said to sit near the driver, and I do. I talk to him sometimes. Other times I read.

Today, going downtown, I read the saddest part of "Little House on the Prairie." The Engel's dog turned around three times and then lay down in his bed and died. I cried on the bus. I was glad I had a handkerchief with me.

The driver asked if I was OK, and I told him the book made me sad because the dog died. He smiled in a kind way.

When I got downtown I bought some beautiful lace for a new doll's dress I am making, and I got an ice cream sundae in the 5 and 10 cent store. This time I got marshmallow sauce instead of whipped cream. It's the same price, and I thought it would be a nice change. And it was!

Next I looked at make-up. The 5 and 10 has two aisles just filled with lipsticks, mascara, nail polish, and lots of other things for women. I had such a good time. I never get bored.

A store like a 5 and 10 is great, 'cause if I get tired in one section I can always find another section to wander around in. And they have a bathroom, which is very important.

Then I waited for the bus to come home, and when it came, guess what? It was the same driver! I was so happy. I sat near him again.

I'm so glad I can do things by my self. I feel so grown-up.

I don't think grownups understand how important it is to do things on your own and not be treated like a baby. I know what I'm doing and I have a brain. I'm lucky my mom and dad let me do a lot on my own.

I have a friend, Shannon. Her parents are very rich, but she never gets to go downtown by herself. She can't believe that I do! They live on my street, but they are moving away next month to a house with ten rooms. Her mother drives her everywhere. I feel sorry for her.

The truth is parents should let their kids do things for themselves.

Dear Diary,

I had to go sleep at my cousin's house again. My older cousin Larry teases me and is not nice. I don't know why he thinks he can tease me just because I'm six years younger.

Once, when I was littler, he told me my spaghetti was really worms. I almost threw up. He makes me very angry.

My mother says, "Maybe he's that way because he doesn't get enough attention from his father."

I really don't care why he's that way. He shouldn't make fun of me and try to trip me when I walk by. It's not right.

14

Dear Diary,

Here is a secret thing I do with my body. I can't help it. It feels so good.

I get a lot of scabs on my knees from roller skating. I kind of like the pain cause it reminds me of how brave I am. In the beginning the scab is really hard and sticks to my skin for a long time. But the day comes when it starts to feel a little loose, and that's when I can't stop checking it. I'm waiting for just the right day when the scab is almost ready to fall off. That's the day I pick it off, and I love that feeling as it comes off my skin.

Well, it's the truth!

Here's a secret about when I grow up. I am going to have two monkeys, two horses, two dogs, two cats and two birds. Oh, and I forgot, six kids.

Right now I just want a dog.

Dear Diary,

I think I just solved another mystery in a Nancy Drew book. I'll finish the book later. I don't want to finish it too fast! I don't know when I'll get my next one. This makes 27 Nancy Drew mystery stories that I've read.

I am so smart! Most of the time I solve the mystery way before the end of the book. I still like to see how Nancy figures it out, though. She has such a fun life.

I'd like to have a life like hers when I'm 17. She gets to do all sorts of stuff by herself. She has a great boyfriend. He is handsome and in love with her. And she has a maid! The maid makes such good food and Nancy is always dressed in such pretty clothing. I love how she looks pretty all the time.

Being smart and pretty are important to me.

Dear Diary,

I don't always think I'm pretty. When I stand next to my cousin Sandra I don't feel pretty. She has perfect looks, and it isn't fair. Once we had a picture taken together, and I thought I looked kind of cute until we got the picture back from being developed. There she was with perfect bangs, shiny hair, a wide movie-star smile, and perfect posture. There I was with messy hair and a slanted smile, and I was not standing straight. I hated her that day. My aunt gave each of us a copy of the picture to keep, but I didn't keep mine. I ripped it up when I got home.

Sometimes I stand in front of the bathroom mirror and look at myself. When I do that I feel pretty.

I have dirty blond hair and brown eyes. My teeth are a little crooked and I have a space between my top two front teeth, but my mother says that makes my smile interesting. I have nice hands. They look good in the mirror, too. I like looking at myself.

Sometimes I hold up my hands in the mirror, like I'm in a commercial selling nail polish. I just kind of smile at myself and hold my hand up so the nails show, and my eyes just shine. Then I move my hand a little, like models do on TV. I really feel special when I'm doing this.

Dear Diary,

I know the truth about looks: The most important thing is to feel pretty. If you feel pretty, then you look pretty. That is the truth for me.

Today Paul looked right at me. He smiled. He was wearing a green sweater. I wish I could hug him and hold hands with him like we were really a couple.

I love him so much.

Dear Diary,

I know a million ways to have fun. I'd better know them, because I feel so rotten when I'm picked last for kickball! I hate standing there on the playground, knowing that each time a name is called I'm closer to the end of the line. Sometimes I just want to die, or better yet, quit school and become a sales lady in the toy department of a department store. But my mother says I can't quit. You have to be at least 16. By that time maybe I'll forget all about kickball.

It makes me so mad to think of Chris and Billy. Those are the two kids that the teacher always picks to choose the teams. I see the gleam in their eyes as they size up who the good players are. They are so mean. Don't they ever think about how I feel, standing there with less and less kids to protect me from the truth that I can't catch the ball so well? I hate them.

Dear Diary,

It's a good thing I have ways to have fun that don't depend on mean kids like Billy and Chris.

I go really fast on my bike down the hill. When I do that, I stand up on the pedals and my hair blows behind me. I imagine I'm a circus rider standing up on her horse, except I'm on a bike.

I roller skate, too. I can roller skate for a long time, even longer than I ride my bike. I love the sensation of rolling along.

But the best thing in the whole world, whether I roller skate a long time or ride my bike, is when I'm done. That's when, if I'm not in a rush to get home, I sit down and smell the skin on my arms. I love the smell after all that exercise. It smells like fresh earth. Sometimes I even lick it. It's so nice and salty.

Dear Diary,

Last night my parents had a big fight. I could sort of hear them through the walls of my room. My eyes were shut tight but my ears were wide open, like elephant ears, trying to hear every word. I couldn't, but they made me nervous and I couldn't sleep. Today in school I was very tired.

I asked my brother this morning if he heard anything and he said, "No." But that doesn't surprise me. He is only six and sleeps like a log. I'm the one that ends up worrying, with my heart pounding so loud I keep thinking it is going to pop out of my chest.

They are the grownups. They shouldn't have stupid fights that keep their child awake. And anyway, nothing gets solved. No one feels better after he is yelled at or put down. No one is going to cooperate any better just because you yell at them and tell them all the things they do are wrong. Even I know that!

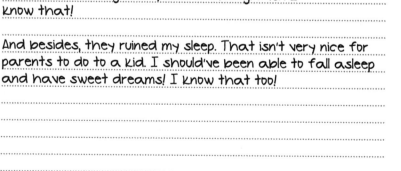

And besides, they ruined my sleep. That isn't very nice for parents to do to a kid. I should've been able to fall asleep and have sweet dreams! I know that too!

21

Dear Diary,

I could teach my mom and dad so much, if only they would listen. Why would a grown-up put down someone he's supposed to love? I don't get it. They waste so much time fighting, and before you know it, everyone's mood is sad or angry and the day is ruined.

This is one thing I'm really promising myself to never do! My dad says, "Don't make a mountain out of a molehill." Well, even though he forgets his own words, I'm going to remember them. 'Cause that is right!

Dear Diary,

I hate Angela and I hope she moves away. She said her parents are buying a new business in upstate New York, and the sooner it happens the better. Yesterday she had the nerve to sit next to Paul. She kept laughing and talking to him, when she knows how in love I am with him. How could she do that to me? We're supposed to be best friends! The whole day in school I had to watch and I felt like I was dying.

I said something to her later, and she said, "What are you talking about? We were just answering the science questions together." Then I thought I better not say anything else, because she might not like me anymore.

Dear Diary,

Paul has been absent for three days. I hope he's not too ill. I miss him so much. I keep thinking about the hill behind his house. Angela told me that kids go there and play "Spin the Bottle." Angela knows everything.

I wonder if Paul knows what goes on up there in the woods. I wish we could play "Spin the Bottle." No I don't. I don't want anyone else to get a chance to kiss him.

Dear Diary,

I hate Gloria. Her teeth are straight, so she'll never need braces. That isn't fair! Also, her thighs are slimmer than mine and don't have little puckers on them. I hate my puckers. At the beach my mom told me to just hold my stomach in and no one will notice my legs. But that is NOT the truth!

The truth is Gloria has nicer legs and she knows it. In dance class she does turns real easy. Who wouldn't with those legs? I guess she'll grow up to be a great dancer and I won't.

I think I'll trip her by accident when she walks by my desk.

Dear Diary,

I like to put on fashion shows in front of the bathroom mirror. I get out some of my mother's clothes and model them. Of course, I make sure my mom isn't home when I do this.

Yesterday I took the beautiful violet velvet dress with the blue Chinese silk shawl that our cousin brought Mom from her trip to China. I put on her high heels and her dangling earrings, the ones she told me Daddy gave her the day I was born. Then I walked into the bathroom like I was a queen. I smiled at myself in the mirror and nodded a little, as I'm saying "Hello" to the crowd. It felt so good.

So far my mother doesn't know I'm taking her things because I'm always careful to put them back exactly where I find them.

Dear Diary,　　　　　　　date: January 10

Today was raining and I had nothing to do. I got out my old fairy tale books. I used to read them all the time but now I only do once in awhile. I wonder what it was really like to be Sleeping Beauty. What did it feel like to be asleep so long and then finally be awakened by a prince kissing you? If I were asleep like that would Paul come along and kiss me? Would he come by on a white horse and scoop me up and throw me on the back of the horse and take me to his palace? Would we go deep into an enchanted forest and then he would love me forever? What if he never came? Could I wake myself up? I sure hope so.

I could teach grownups so much if only they would listen. Lots of times they pretend to listen and then they answer you, but they haven't really heard what you said or asked. They think they are off the hook just because they answered.

They aren't off the hook.

Dear Diary,

Why do grown-ups fight over stupid things? I don't get it. Before you know it, everyone's mood is bad and the day is ruined. Like I remember last summer — we never made it to the lake because Daddy kept yelling at Mom about the dent in the car and telling her she was stupid for parking the way she did in front of the drugstore. I even heard him say, "Of all the women in the world, I get to marry the most stupid." I think Mommy is smart. It made me feel so sick in my head to hear Daddy talk like that.

Daddy finally rushed out of the house and took the car, and Mommy went into the bedroom. I think she was crying.

We kids just sat there all droopy in our bathing suits. I was sweating and cold at the same time. It was awful.

Dear Diary,

I know I am very smart! Smart people solve mysteries and add numbers fast and realize if someone is lying. So I know I'm smart. And that's the truth.

Some of the Nancy Drew Mysteries I solved before Nancy solved them:

1. The Scarlet Slipper Mystery
(two chapters before Nancy solved it)
2. The Ringmaster's Secret
(the page before she solved it)
3. The Clue Of The Velvet Mask
(three chapters earlier!)
4. The Mystery At The Ski Jump
(same page but first!)
5. The Clue Of The Black Keys
(five pages earlier)
6. The Secret Of The Wooden Lady
(I forget)
7. The Clue Of The Leaning Chimney
(about seven pages)

Dear Diary,

I'm so excited. Today in the mail there was a package for me from Aunt Belinda. She lives in Colorado and I hardly ever see her, but she always remembers me. Last year she sent me this diary that I'm writing in now. I wonder what she sent me this year. Since my birthday is still two weeks away I'm not going to open the package yet. I think I'll hide it in my underwear drawer. I like to have mysteries, even if I make them up myself! Now I have "The Mystery of the Unopened Package."

Dear Diary,

A list of things I know how to do:
(list not finished)
I know how to clean the house.
I know how to do laundry.
I know how to iron.
I know how to cut and make doll clothing from patterns,
and I know how to design outfits for them even without a
pattern. I have a special way to cut the tops for their
clothes so all I have to do is sew a snap and they stay
on!
I know how to tidy up the house.
I know how to cook.
I know how to draw.
I know how to get into the house when I
forget the back door key: Mom keeps a key
on the inside of the door. I have to push it
out of the lock onto a piece of newspaper
and then wiggle the newspaper under the
door until the key slides under the door to
the outside.
I know how to read hard books.
I know how to play the piano and make up music on the
black keys, even though I never took any lessons. The
music sounds Chinese. I think I'm the only person who plays
on the black keys—at least the only one not living in China!

Dear Diary,

I know how to raise a lot of children; maybe even a dozen like in "Cheaper by the Dozen." I know because I take very good care of my dolls and I am very loving and very good to people and to animals.

I can lift my brother and he weighs a lot.

I can ride my bike for hours and go really fast downhill.

I can roller-skate and ice-skate.

I can do summersaults and bend over backwards.

I can dance and I can make up steps.

Dear Diary,

I'm worried. I really think I want to be a ballet dancer, but I have trouble turning and that might mean I can't be a dancer. The teacher says that turns are a must. I hope she's wrong.

I'm going to try harder like I did with ice-skating. I made myself stand on the ice in my ice skates and practice, even with my ankles caving in, until I could skate just like the other kids!

Dear Diary,

More things I can do:
I can make potholders, and they are good to sell for
spending money.
I can embroider.
I can knit.

Dear Diary,

I saw Paul's mother today. She brought his lunch into the classroom. She looks very nice. She had on lipstick and a really nice sweater set. It was blue.

I tried to look really special when she was in the room. I sat up really straight and raised my hand. No one else had their hand up. I didn't know what I would say if the teacher called on me. But she didn't anyway. I wonder if Mrs. Fein noticed me. I hope so!

Dear Diary,

I have a new good friend. We have fun together. I got to sleep over Dawn's house, and we talked until late at night and laughed really hard.

Her house feels funny compared to mine. Her parents don't say much to me and her mother smokes. Their rooms seem darker. I think it's because they have dark drapes on the windows. I don't know what the smell is in the house. It's a little yucky, though.

But I still like to go there because we tell secrets and sometimes talk about grown-up stuff, like boys. We even look at each other's chest to see if anything is happening yet.

It isn't.

Dear Diary,

I just finished reading Black Beauty yesterday. I've been crying on and off for days while reading it, and as I finished the book I cried for two hours straight. My nose was so stuffed up, I had to take nose drops just to breathe again. My dad asked me why I was crying so much. I told him it was because people are so mean to animals.

Why are people so cruel? Black Beauty was such a kind, wonderful horse. How could anyone ever think of making him into soap? I can't stand it.

Dear Diary,

What is wrong with human beings? I had to read THE DIARY OF ANNE FRANK in Sunday school and again I felt so horrible. She died only a few years older than I am. And she loved life so much. How can it be?

I want to scream out to the whole world, "Stop being mean! Start caring!"

I promise I'll never forget you, Black Beauty! Your spirit lives on through me.

My parents love me but they don't understand the things that make me suffer. Even Daddy didn't really understand about Black Beauty. He just hugged me and gave me more Kleenex and told me to go to bed.

Dear Diary,

My parents hurt me so much by fighting with each other. I don't really know why they fight, but when I hear Daddy say that he is going to take his suitcase down and go and stay at Grandma's, I get really scared and sad. I lie in bed and my heart just pounds. How can I get enough sleep to go to school and be able to think?

What is there to fight about so late at night? The truth is that you should try to get along! They put each other down, even sometimes calling each other names. This is not right. Why don't they stop?

I pray at night that they will stop fighting someday soon!

39

Dear Diary,

I still watch Paul all the time. I am still sure that this is love. I imagine us together, swimming and then lying in the sun on a towel and looking into each other's eyes.

I know my body will be different someday. Sometimes I stand in front of the mirror and lean over so my chest turns into breasts and I look grown-up.

I don't know all the stuff that is going to happen over the next few years, but I do know that I want to marry Paul someday.

Dear Diary,

Today is my birthday. My grandparents and my grandaunts sent me money in envelopes. I got $100.00 all together. I'm going to get a new bike with the money. The bike I want has three speeds and it is dark shiny blue. It is an English bicycle. I guess that means it is the kind they ride in England. Anyway, my mom will take me to pick it up tomorrow when she gets home from work. I'm so excited. I have never used speeds before.

We had cake and ice cream for dessert tonight and steak for supper. The steak was so tender, and I got the bone. My dad usually gets the bone, but it is my birthday! They sang Happy Birthday to me and my grandparents came over after dinner for dessert. Everyone hugged and kissed me.

Grandma asked me if Aunt Belinda had sent me a present. I said, "Yes." She said, "Well, what was it?"

I felt embarrassed. I said, "Wait a minute. I have to go to the bathroom."

I raced upstairs and ran to my underwear drawer. There it was. The unopened package. I ripped it open. It was a gold locket on a chain. It was so beautiful, in the shape of a heart. And on the front was an engraved design.

Dear Diary,

The locket opens and has space for two pictures. Aunt Belinda had put a picture of me in one of the openings. The other was blank. I love it!

Her note said, "To my precious niece. Happy Birthday and Many More. Love, Aunt Belinda."

I raced around my room so excited, holding the locket right up to my heart. Then I put it on. Then I flushed the toilet so my grandmother would think I really went to the bathroom. Then I went back downstairs.

"That's a lovely locket. Isn't it nice, in the shape of a heart? And how sweet. It opens! What a beautiful picture of you. I wonder who you will put in the other side. Maybe your brother? Wear it in good health."

Grandma hugged me again and slipped into my hand another $5.00 bill.

I had a wonderful day. Except I know I'll never put my brother on the other side!

Dear Diary,

Paul and I are the same height now. I grew this year and he didn't. My mother says that is common at my age.

I liked it when he was taller than me. But I still love him.

Dear Diary,

My mother told me not to expect to marry Paul. That makes me angry because he is the person I love. I don't think she understands that.

Every day I know how I feel just looking at him. He is the smartest boy in the room, and I can't imagine growing up and not being with him. I would rather die.

I am in love!

Dear Diary,

Today my feelings were hurt.

In class I raise my hand a lot. I have so many questions to ask. Miss Shannon was talking about the wheel and how it changed so many things in the world when it was invented. I raised my hand and asked what the world might have been like if something else had been invented instead of the wheel. She just looked at me with her really sharp grey eyes and said, "Now, isn't that silly!" Then she turned to everyone else and asked them to think of other inventions that depend on the wheel.

It bothers me that Miss Shannon doesn't like my questions. Sometimes she doesn't call on me at all, and I know she sees my hand waving. That makes me feel bad inside.

But I don't give up, even if I have a funny feeling around my heart when she ignores me. I still raise my hand the next time I have a question.

Dear Diary,

Things for Grownups to Remember:
Don't be mean to animals.
Try not to swear for a month.
Don't fight with anyone you love.
Don't put people down or call them names.
Believe your child if she tells you she is in love.
Answer a kid's questions.
Listen to their ideas.

Dear Diary,

The most fun I think I have ever had so far in my life was being in the school play last week. I didn't have the biggest part, but I knew from the time I got it that I was going to do a great job, and I did.

The way I felt as I said my lines was so wonderful. I could feel my whole body, as if it got as big as the moon. I could feel the pressure inside of me pushing me to "be" the princess in the story, to feel her very being. I knew my connection with her and her feelings would come through.

And it did. I was so good. I knew as the words came out of my mouth that my voice sounded great and my face looked like the princess I was supposed to be, and I knew that afterward people would come up to me and compliment me. And boy, did they!

I was surrounded by everyone. Several people told me I should be an actress. I loved all the attention. My parents gave me flowers and my dad took my picture. I looked good in the picture, in my long dress that was what a princess would wear. But the picture couldn't show how I was flying inside.

I will never forget that night.

I could be much prettier if my mom would let me use make-up. When I was in the school play I got to wear a long dress and make-up. I could tell by looking at myself how make-up makes a big difference with me.

My mom says it's because I have such sallow skin and black rings under my eyes from allergies. I think she is right.

I have to wait to wear make-up at least two more years. That's a long time not to look my best.

I wonder if Paul would notice if I wore makeup.

I wear my locket all the time. I love to touch it while I'm in school. It feels so good when I rub it with my fingers. I like to touch the engraving too. It goes round and round in a circle that never seems to end.

I wonder how I can get Paul's picture? I want to put his picture in the other side of the locket. After all, isn't that what you do when you have a sweetheart? I love him so much. If I could have his picture in my locket it would be almost like we were really a couple.

Maybe I could get his school picture? How would I ever get it? And besides, it is much too big for the locket. My parents have a Brownie camera but they would never let me just take it to school. This is a big problem.

Maybe I'm not so good at solving mysteries after all. I wish Nancy Drew could help me.

Dear Diary,

I can be so miserable at home. Usually it is when my parents start fighting. But if I can get away from them, then I'm okay. When I stay around and listen, I feel like they are yelling at me. But once I can get away then it's like I come alive again. I get on my bike or roller skates or I walk down the hill to my friend's house, and then I feel okay.

I'm still sad for them and angry that they waste time fighting, but at least I'm in a good mood again.

These last few weeks of school have been wonderful. Guess why? Miss Shannon got sick and we have the greatest substitute. His name is Mr. Reid and he's fun and also nice. He told us he just finished becoming a teacher. I can't believe how different school has been. We made butter from milk by churning it by hand and we had crackers and butter. We made candles with real string and melted wax. He brought us all jump ropes and taught us how to exercise outside. He has a rule that we can't play anything where we choose sides until the last kid is chosen. CAUSE IT HURTS FEELINGS! He actually said that. I love him. And he always calls on me when my hand is up. Five times so far he told me what a great answer I gave. Three times he said the question I asked was terrific. I am feeling so good!

Good bye Miss Shannon. I will never forget you, Mr. Reid.

Dear Diary,

I won't be seeing Paul over the summer. He said he's going away to camp. Maybe he'll miss me. I know I'll miss him terribly. I can't imagine him not being nearby. I am lonely already. How will I get through each day?

I HATE to go to the city camp. My parents are making me go and I have to drag my brother also. Yuck. Twice a week they make us swim in that awful "Y" pool that smells of chlorine, and they also try to teach us tennis. I hate tennis. I always miss the ball. And they have the most boring arts and crafts. I don't want to make another wallet. What will I do with another wallet? I have five from last summer.

Dear Diary,

I wish I could travel. I think it's so neat to meet new people, and seeing new things really is like getting a present.

I know when I grow up I'm going to travel a lot, and that's the truth.

The biggest trip I ever had so far was when we went to Florida in a big plane to the town where my Aunt Nelly lives. My aunt and uncle have a cute little ranch house. Of course we had to stay with them, so I didn't have a chance to stay in a big hotel. I got to stay in the finished basement, so I can imagine how much I would feel like a princess if we could stay in a big hotel. "Hello room service? Please bring me a dish of coffee ice cream, with jimmies on it."

My parents let me go up in a tiny plane by myself (well the pilot was there too) while we were there. The plane ride was wonderful. I was scared and there wasn't even a roof on the plane. I was just sitting there behind the pilot with the wind pushing my hair in my eyes.

The pilot was so handsome. My heart was pounding from fright when the plane went really high. The pilot turned to me and said I could hold his hand if I was scared.

Dear Diary,

So guess what! While we were swooping over the houses and over the orange groves, I held his hand. It felt so reassuring and I felt so much like Nancy Drew at the same time. I wonder if he thought I looked older, maybe 16.

My parents down below looked tiny, tiny, tiny. When we came back and landed they were waving and throwing me kisses, and my mom looked like she was crying. When I came down to earth again it was one of those really special moments when my mom and dad and I were all so happy together. They were happy I was alive and hadn't crashed, and I was happy I got to hold the pilot's hand and feel like I was 16.

It was a perfect day, and that's the truth.

Dear Diary,

Angela, Betty, Joanne, Karen, Dorothy, Dawn, and I came up with a way to get through the summer. We meet at our houses once a week and trade books. It is a club. A book trading club. That way we all get more books to read. We are trading mostly Nancy Drew, Trixie Belden, Cherry Ames and a few others, books like "Rebecca of Sunny Brook Farms" and "Little House on the Prairie."

Of course, my favorite is still Nancy Drew, but now I think I might want to be a nurse after reading Cherry Ames.

Yesterday we met at Dorothy's house. She has a color television in her living room. No one else has one. After we traded books, we watched the Mickey Mouse Club and then pretended we were the different kids on the show. We were laughing and having fun singing the Mickey Mouse song and making up dances. Dorothy's mother finally came into the room and told us we had to stop, we might break something.

I had so much fun. Angela and I were still singing as we walked home.

Next week we meet at my house. I'm going to bake brownies. My mom said she'll teach me the recipe she used when she was 12.

I'm so excited.

Dear Diary,

I know if you keep putting your face into expressions where you look mean and angry and irritated, your face is going to stay looking that way. If instead you keep putting your face into beautiful shapes where you're smiling, laughing, and looking happy, then you'll stay looking more that way as you get older.

Dear Diary,

A lot of people don't seem to know the truth about color. Everybody looks better in certain colors than other colors and certain styles than other styles.

I have sallow skin and certain colors don't look good on me: yellow is "yucky awful." Other colors, like pink and certain shades of beautiful bright blue, look wonderful on me. I don't have a lot of clothes but I know the truth, and I'll know how to dress when I get older.

I know a lot of truth about health too.

When I feel good I go for long bike rides and I stay outside a lot and I roller-skate, and when I'm sick I stay inside and rest. I get sick a lot because I have big tonsils. My mother told me I might have to have them out one day. I don't want to. She tried to make it sound okay by telling me I would have tons of ice cream after they take them out. I'm not a baby! What about the pain and being put to sleep? That's the real stuff. I hope they can stay.

Anyway, you shouldn't make yourself do things when you feel sick, and when you feel well you should do a lot of things, because that's the truth!

Dear Diary,

I know the truth about friends.

Some people make you feel creepy, and they always make you feel bad. The truth is you shouldn't hang around with them. Some people make you feel wonderful, Dorothy makes me feel like that, and you should hang around with them instead.

If you don't have anyone good to hang around with, then hang around with yourself!

Dear Diary,

I'm most happy when no one is fighting and no one is telling me what's wrong with me. I think that is the truth for just about everybody, and that's why I love being with my grandparents. We have a lot of fun and they don't ever criticize me. They like everything about me just the way I am. They even put that stupid picture of me, the one with my bangs cut off, up on the mantle place and keep telling everyone how beautiful I am.

When my grandparents take me out, my mother stays home and rests. I'm really happy because it's so perfect. They get me ice cream, even if I already had one a couple of hours ago, and they take me to beautiful parks where we feed peanuts to the birds. One of the parks has flying horses, and sometimes they let me go on ten rides.

It's wonderful to be so happy. And all it takes is people who love you, don't criticize you, and don't pick fights over anything.

And that's the truth!

60

Dear Diary,

I'm also very happy when I'm eating. The most fun way to eat is with others that care about me.

When I'm with other people I don't pig out like I do when I eat a giant Hershey Bar alone in my bedroom. I sit up straight, mind my manners, and put my napkin in my lap, and I don't eat all hunched over.

When I'm with my three aunts, the stories they tell are amazing! They are really old, so I get to hear all about what it was like when they grew up: how they had a seamstress who made all the children's clothes, how the trolley went right by their house, and how they had only one phone in a closet under the stairway in the front hall. The telephone didn't have a dial on it. When you had to make a call, you picked the receiver up and told the operator you wanted to make a call. Then the operator rang the person you wanted to talk to.

I love hearing about the old days.

Dear Diary,

My aunts always take me to the Sunshine Café. We order sandwiches, like egg salad, tuna, or cream cheese and olives, without the crusts. Then we get coffee Jell-O with whipped cream for dessert. Everything is so delicious. I eat while they chat about what new dresses they need to purchase and where they are going on vacation. They always tell me how adorable I look and how pretty my haircut is and how smart I am.

The truth is lunch out with my aunts is the very best way in the whole world to eat.

The Club met at my house today. Thank goodness my brother was next door playing. He is such a pest. He probably would have ruined everything. I set the table in the dining room and my mother let me put Grandma's plates out for the brownies. We have six of them and they all have painted flowers on them. My mother said they came from Austria and they are very expensive. All the girls were so careful. I put a little sign on the table that said, "Be Careful."

The brownies I made were delicious. I ate four of them. Here's the recipe so I'll never forget it:

RECIPE

2 squares of unsweetened chocolate. Yuk!

½ cup Crisco

1 ¼ cup sugar

3 eggs

¾ cup flour

½ teaspoon baking powder

½ teaspoon salt

½ cup chopped nuts, I put in much more

I mixed everything, but first I had to melt the chocolate over hot water. Everything got baked for ½ hour at 350 degrees. I put coconut and colored sprinkles on top. (I made that part up.)

Dear Diary,

Tomorrow we go back to school. I know Paul is home because I walked by his house and saw his bicycle in the driveway. I can't wait to see him. I wonder if he grew over the summer. I hope so. I think I still love him.

I try to remember his eyes and how they make me feel all funny inside.

Dear Diary,

I get in bad moods a lot. My mother says that's because I'm growing and changing. She says I'll probably get my period soon. I hope not. I hope it waits as long as possible.

I don't really want to grow up right now. There are a lot of things I like about being my age. I can do a lot of things that grownups do, but I don't have their responsibilities or problems. I don't have to make money and I don't have to involve myself in family troubles like my parents have to. They are always either fighting with each other or worried about the health of their parents or discussing money, and I don't have to do things like that.

I worry about my parents because they don't know the truth about so many things and they still fight over stupid stuff. When will they ever grow up?

Dear Diary,

Our teacher is nice. Her name is Mrs. Gamble.

Paul is even smaller than I remembered. I guess I grew even more over the summer than I realized.

I'm sitting in the same row he is, so it's harder to look at him all the time, because I have to turn my head.

The good news is Angela is in the row in back of me, not next to him. I'm not worried about her anymore.

Dear Diary,

Today when I came out of the shower, I lifted my arm in front of the mirror as I was drying myself. I had three dark hairs growing from my right armpit! I can't believe it. It's beginning.

Good news: Nothing in the other armpit yet.

Dear Diary,

When I wake up in the morning I look at my wallpaper and try to see pictures in it that I have never seen before. There are flowers and birds, but sometimes I can see other things, like animals or faces. Doing that puts me in a good mood.

Then, before I get out of bed I think of something good that will happen that day. I might get to watch I LOVE LUCY or get to eat the chocolate cake left over from yesterday in the kitchen. As long as there is something that I know will make today a good day, I'm happy.

Dear Diary,

Even if I'm sick I can think of good things. I'll think about cutting out some new paper dolls or reading some more in my latest Nancy Drew Mystery book. Even the day I threw up all day and had to go to the bathroom all day, I cheered myself up by lying on my parents' bed and reading a mystery book. I put pillows all around me and brought in my baby doll. I felt sick, but I felt nice and cozy.

There's always a way to make things better!

Dear Diary,

If I could run away, these are some of the places I would run to: I'd run to the prairie to live with Laura Ingalls because her family is so loving and they always have things to do and things to look forward to. When they have worries, they have real worries. Their problems are real problems that they have to solve, not exaggerated nothings like someone getting angry over some tiny stupid thing. I would feel special living with them. Even if I have to eat potatoes all winter, like they did one year, I'd go and live with them.

Another family I'd go live with is the "Cheaper by the Dozen" family. They have so much fun. They have so many brothers and sisters and they put on plays and they get to learn languages even when they're sitting on the toilet.

You know where else I'd go and live? I'd go to I LOVE LUCY and I'd be her daughter. Ethel and Fred would be our neighbors. We'd get into so many silly predicaments, and even though Desi might get angry at me, he'd always laugh and hug me at the end. We'd have fun. We'd go to California and I'd get to see some of the Hollywood movie stars. I'd sit by the pool and they'd introduce me as their beautiful daughter. Then if I wanted to be a star they'd help me become one.

Dear Diary,

There's a special song that sometimes floats into my head that is so uplifting; it gives me a funny feeling somewhere down around my heart and stomach, like a magic tickle. I love it, but I don't know what it is and no one can identify it. It's as if I recognize it from a long time ago. Every once in awhile it comes back to me. It just enters my brain and I get that good feeling. I'm beginning to think I know that song from maybe before I was born.

I've tried to sing it aloud to lots of people, but no one recognizes it. I hope I can remember this song as I get older. The last time it came to me, my mom and I were walking downtown. She was taking me to get a new dress. I sang it for her, but she still didn't know it.

So this is really a puzzle, but it is still a truth that strange things can make us happy.

Dear Diary,

I don't know if I want to be a teenager because they're so obsessed about make-up and clothing and giggling and flirting with boys. I've been in love, but my love is really very grown-up. I don't do all that crazy laughing and hysterical stuff. I don't even chase Paul. If I could just marry Paul now or in a couple of years, say when I'm fourteen, like my great grandmother who got married at that age, it would be so wonderful. We would have babies and make a family and not fight. We'd just love each other.

I don't know if I want to go through all the stuff I read about in the "True Confessions" magazine that my cousin Ruth hid under her mattress. It had awful stories about fighting and babies that came even though the girl wasn't married.

When I told my mother about it, she just said not to read that trash magazine ever again. I won't, but I needed more help than she gave. I don't think she understands how frightened I am.

I don't want to leave behind everything I know now and become some hysterical teenager who gets in trouble!

Dear Diary,

I don't understand why teenage girls aren't more like Nancy Drew. She's a teenager but she doesn't go around laughing hysterically and getting silly and wasting time. She's busy solving mysteries and helping people. She's curious and she follows up on clues and she takes things very seriously, but she still has fun. She has a boyfriend and wears pretty clothes.

I don't get it. What happens to girls when they are older than me? Do they drink some kind of magic potion that makes them not have any brains? I hope I never drink that drink. I like my brain and I like to feel smart.

I need help. I don't know who to turn to for this help. My mother and father? I don't think they can help me with the things I'm feeling.

The truth is, I'm afraid to ask, so they really don't know I have these worries. I don't know why I am afraid to talk about them, I just am.

Dear Diary,

I am afraid of dying. What happens to you? Where was I before I was born? And how can I remember after I die all that happened to me when I was alive? What if it hurts to die? And what if I die too soon, before I can do all the things I want to do?

How can I stay alive forever?

I'm worried, what if my mother or father or grandmother or grandfather die? I couldn't stand it. I would go out of my mind. How can you go on living if people you love die? My whole life is my parents and grandparents. I can't even imagine existing without them. I even told my parents that if they try to go on a vacation without me I'll hide in the trunk of their car.

I wish somebody could help me with these worries.

My dad has been interviewing for a new job. If he gets it, we'll have to move away, not that far but far enough. I won't see anyone I know again. At least I won't see people unless we make a really special effort and I don't know if my parents will do that.

One good thing is I won't have to go to my cousin's house anymore and be teased. Another thing is we'll have a bigger house, big enough for a dog.

But I have this kind of scary feeling about leaving. I'm so used to this house, even the bushes that separate our house from the Gleason's. I know everything around here, where everything is and who everyone is.

Although I'm scared I'm willing to try. Of course it's going to be hard to leave Paul here. I'll never forget him, but if we're meant to be he'll find me! My mother keeps telling me that there'll be other boys. I think I finally believe her. I need someone to love me. Staring at Paul is not enough for me anymore.

My father will have a really good job where he'll get more money and people will look up to him. I think that's going to be good. No more hand-me-downs from my cousins! I think maybe my parents will fight less because my father will feel better about himself.

Even grownups have to feel good, or they get really cranky, and that's the truth.

Dear Diary,

When I get older how can I still be me and have to do things that I don't want to do, like put all my dolls away and wear a bra? How will I feel about my body when I have to wear a pad? (I don't even want to write the word, let alone say it aloud.) How will I still be me?

The next thing that worries me is how will I get to do all the things I want to do?

The last thing that worries me is how will I ever convince my parents to get me a pet? They keep saying no. They don't realize how much this hurts me. I really need something of my own to love. I can't keep sleeping with my dolls when I'm thirteen. That would look stupid.

Dear Diary,

Angela told me EVERYTHING about growing up when she slept over my house last Friday night. At least everything she learned from her mother. We got into our pajamas and under the covers. We had to whisper and keep the light off so my mother would think we were asleep. We kept giggling. Some things I knew, but lots I didn't. I felt ok about most of the stuff.

But I was still crying a little inside because I want to be able to talk to my mother the way she can talk to her mom. I'm so jealous.

Angela said she thought it was time I should definitely ask my mother for a training bra. It is never too soon, she said. Mrs. Allen is getting her one next week. I guess she saw my chest when we got undressed.

I know I'm bigger than I used to be but what is there to train?

Dear Diary,

Today I was up in my room dancing to a rock 'n' roll song on the radio. I was getting so hot and sweaty and really going wild. It felt great!

My mom came to the door and suddenly opened it. I thought she would get mad cause my room was a mess and I was in bare feet. But instead she grinned and came in and started dancing with me. She even took a fake long-stemmed rose and held it between her teeth, like they do in movies when the woman is dancing the tango. She actually knows how to dance! I couldn't believe it.

We danced like crazy for two more songs. Then she collapsed onto my bed and pulled me down with her and we hugged. She looked happier than I've seen her in ages. She told me that she used to dance in her bedroom when she was a kid, and she would hold her hairbrush in her hand like a microphone and pretend to sing.

I was so happy today. I hope we dance together again soon.

Dear Diary,

I'm at least four inches taller than Paul now. That bothers me. I still love him, but I'm discouraged.

My dad got the job. He told us at dinner. We'll be moving in June. I felt sort of numb when he told us.

Mom said we can come back and visit, because we're only moving two towns away.

Still, it won't be the same. Ever.

Dear Diary,

You're not going to believe this. I walked into the living room and Daddy was crying. He told me that his brother was sick and had to have an operation. He was very worried. I asked Daddy if he was praying to God, and he said no. He wasn't sure that that would help. That made me feel very funny inside, like a big giant pit was opening up in the bottom of my stomach.

Doesn't my father know that I need God? I need my dad to believe in Him. How can he say that he's not sure?

Now he's scared me, and that's the truth.

Dear Diary,

I'm heartsick because I don't think Paul loves me. I send him signals all day long. I look at him as much as possible. I still feel all the same feelings inside. This must be true love because it has lasted so long, even with him being shorter than I am. But I have to admit I'm getting discouraged.

I really hoped, since I pray to God every night, even though Paul's a kid and my mother says that boys don't fall in love and that they don't even care about girls, that he would be different. I keep hoping that he can show his love for me even though he's a kid.

The pain is so immense I want to die — except if I die now, I'll never get a dog, and Mom hinted I might be getting one when we move. She almost promised when I told her I felt so funny about moving. She said that was normal.

I don't like that part of being normal.

Dear Diary,

Paul behaves like I'm not even there. Do you think I stare at him too much? Oh, Paul, look at me, love me. I am sitting right near you totally in love! And tonight when I lie in bed I'll be imagining us getting older and being boyfriend and girlfriend for real.

I wonder what kind of dog they'll get me? I love poodles.

I still wear my locket all the time. I never did put Paul's picture in it, though.

I'm miserable.

Dear Diary,   date: May 28

Angela, Dorothy, and all the girls gave me a party today at Betty's at our last Club meeting. They brought me gifts.

Dorothy brought me a beautiful diary to write in. Maybe I'll use it when we move.

Angela gave me a gift certificate to the book store in my new town. Her mother must have driven her there to get it. That was so sweet.

Dawn gave me a bracelet with a heart that is engraved with my name. I can wear it sometimes when I wear my locket.

Betty's mom made us supper. We had macaroni and tuna casserole, peas, and homemade apple pie. Then we had peanut butter cups, four each. I love the way peanut butter cups feel in my mouth. Betty's mom is the best. I'll never forget today. I'm glad Betty's mom took our picture. She said she'll send me a copy.

I wonder if I'll really see all the girls again after I move.

Dear Diary,

I don't want to stay home during the day when I grow up. I'm going to really be somebody when I'm older. I'm not going to let anybody trap me inside a house with nothing to do but chores and laundry. I'll get the right education. If I'm going to be an actress then I'll get that training. If I'm going to be something else, I'll do whatever it takes. I'm not going to be outside with the clothes basket, hanging the clothes. My kids can hang the wash while I do more important things.

I'm going to be somebody. And that's the truth.

Dear Diary,

My mother just told me that she is expecting a baby in five months. I can't believe it! I am not happy.

My brother and I had everything worked out. We don't need to share with anyone else or to take care of a baby! And we are moving. I'll have so much on my mind: a new school, a new house, and new friends. I'll be busy taking care of my new poodle, I hope!

Now, I'll have to listen to a baby crying at night! And maybe help.

No, this is not fair! Did my mom want this baby? I wish I could ask, but I can't.

I know she would just look away and fidget or just walk into the other room. I guess my mom thinks I can't understand the truth. But I can!

Dear Diary,

Next week we're moving. I've been packing like crazy for the last six weeks. My parents don't know how to pack, but I do, so I've kind of been in charge. I'm good at that. There're boxes everywhere. I'm kind of excited and I'm kind of scared.

I went on a bike ride around the neighborhood today. I looked at the big tree that I always climb, and I said good bye to it. I rode to the drug store and had maybe my last coffee ice cream cone. I rode down the hill really, really fast one last time. I even went to the other end of the street where I usually don't go, just so I can remember all the houses for the entire four blocks that are our street.

You should see my new house! It's bigger and it's all one floor with three bathrooms. I never thought we'd live in a house with three bathrooms! It has a back porch and a big yard. The last family who lived there left a swing so I can swing out there. It's in a very pretty neighborhood. I'll be turning twelve within a few months of living in this house.

I'm excited because I'm going to meet all new friends.

Dear Diary,

I forgot to tell you we had our school dance and Paul asked me to dance twice. He didn't ask anyone else to dance more than once, so I was very happy.

It was funny dancing with him, he being so much shorter than I am. I couldn't even look into his eyes. I just looked over his head, across the gym to the walls. But I still felt a little tingling in my body being that near to him.

I don't think I feel quite so much in love as I always thought I was. I don't think I'll put his picture in my locket now. I'm not sure what I'll put in there.

Dear Diary,

When we move I'll be busy with a new school and new friends. There's so much to look forward to.

I'm not as scared of getting older now. I don't know why exactly. I wasn't even upset when I lifted my arms and saw too many hairs to bother to count.

I feel a little rush of excitement, different than falling in love with Paul. But just as good.

I've decided that when we move I'm not going to set up all my dolls on the bureau. I'm going to put some of them away carefully in boxes along with their clothes. I'm also not going to take all of my comic books to the new house. I've begun to sort them out. I'm giving away the ones for kids, like "Donald Duck" and "Little Lulu."

I'll keep just one "Little Lulu" to remember.

Dear Diary,

I wonder if I'll be able to sleep tonight. The movers are coming at 8:00 tomorrow morning! This is the prayer I am going to say to God tonight, because we are moving tomorrow:

Dear God, I hope our move is safe and good and we'll all be happy in our new house. Please help my parents to fight less. Help me to remember forever the truth, even when I grow up. When I have children, let our house be filled with laughter and fun. When my kids ask me questions, help me to tell them the truth. And help me to never forget the tiny things, like licking the salt off my skin after I sweat. Help me to know how to dress and how to keep my face looking soft, and also, can you help me become a teenager without being too afraid? Help me not to feel bad about leaving behind what I have to leave behind.

Dear Diary,   date: June 27

The movers are coming in 20 minutes.

I finally decided what I want to put into my locket. I'm
putting a tiny slip of paper that has on it things I don't
want to forget. I might have to write in code because it is
so small. But I'll know how to break the code. That's
because I'm smart — just like Nancy Drew.

I decided my secret reminder is more important than a
picture of Paul. I'll never forget him, of course, but the
secret I'm putting inside the locket is for me forever. I'll
wear my locket next to my heart. The words will face my
face when the locket is closed, so I'll always
remember The Truth.

Dear Diary,   (date:)

Things I promise to do when I grow up:

I'll travel a lot.

I won't look away when my kids ask me tough questions.

I'll answer truthfully.

I won't swear.

I won't get into silly fights with my husband.

I'll have fun with my kids and laugh a lot.

I'll remember ME!

And that's
the Truth!

Questions For Kids

1. What do you think happens right after the book ends?

2. What do you think about the girl in The Truth?

3. What did you like about her?

4. What didn't you like?

5. Did you ever feel like her?

6. Did she teach you anything?

7. Do you know anyone like the girl?

8. If you do, what is she like?

9. Would you like to have a friend like her?

10. What would you like to tell the girl?

11. What do you think she would say to you?

12. Are there any secrets you would tell her?

13. Do you think she had other secrets that she didn't put in her diary?

14. How is she different from you?

15. How is she the same as you?

16. What was your favorite page?

17. What was the funniest part of The Truth?

18. Are there important things she didn't talk about?

19. What made you angry in the book? Sad? Happy?

20. What do you want to remember most when you grow up?

21. What do you wish your parents better understood about you?

22. Would you like your mother and/or father to read this book?

23. Is there a part of The Truth that you would like to talk to your mother or father about?

24. If you could give the girl a name, what would you name her?

25. Would you like to write to the girl? If you would like to write to her, here is the address to use: drbarbara@enchantedself.com

To all the wonderful mothers, aunts, grandmothers, teachers, and friends of "The Girl," who just read this book:

As a positive psychologist and a woman, it has been a pleasure for me to bring *The Truth, I'm A Girl, I'm Smart and I Know Everything!* to your girl. I hope "The Girl" was fun and meaningful to your youngster. I hope you also had a chance to read the book, and to have your mind and heart opened by "The Girl."

I am here for all of you! I would love to come to your child's school to speak to the children and/or to the PTA about issues raised in the book. I would also be delighted to come to your book club, women's club or other organization to discuss our journeys from girlhood to womanhood in meaningful, fun, and inspiring ways.

And don't forget the virtual world. I would also be happy to visit your child's school and/or your book club or woman's group via speaker phone, teleconferencing, and/or video cam.

Let's keep the discussion going. Remember, we were once all little princesses. We all had a sense of "The Truth" and of our power and talents. My dream is that we all pass on "The Truth." Our little princesses will thank us! And the little princess inside of each of us will glow knowing that we ourselves are courageous enough never to forget!

Please contact me at drbarbara@enchantedself.com or 732-571-1200. Please come and visit me at www.thetruthforgirls.com and www.enchantedself.com

And of course, I am available to you for workshops, retreats, virtual classes, speaking engagements, and radio and television appearances.

Books by Dr. Barbara Becker Holstein:

The Enchanted Self, A Positive Therapy

Recipes For Enchantment, The Secret Ingredient is YOU!

Delight

Delight
CD-rom version with art, music and voice

Feel Good Stories
Edited by Dr. Holstein and written by her mother, Bernice Becker

The Truth, I'm Ten, I'm Smart and I Know Everything!
Adult Women's Version of The Truth

These books are available through Amazon.com,
all other on-line bookstores, and your local bookstore.
Look for them on www.enchantedself.com.